Dreaming

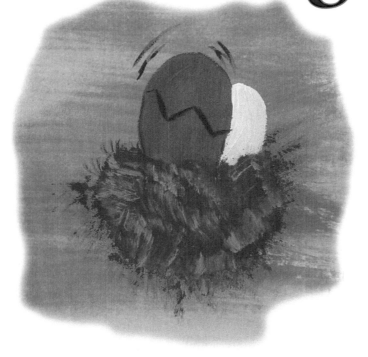

by Tom Leggott & Jenni Corbett
Illustrated by Jenni Corbett

First published in Australia in 2014
by Lilly Pilly Publishing
www.lillypillypublishing.com
lillypillypublishing@outlook.com

Story editing and layout: Julieann Wallace

Tom Leggot & Jenni Corbett
Dreaming 1st Edition
For children 4 +
ISBN: 978-0-9942044-1-7 (paperback)

Designed by Lilly Pilly Publishing

Lilly Pilly Publishing

To those people who forced us out of our comfort zone and to Russell Island.
To friends and family who have
inspired the characters of the Tourist Birds - no malicious intent is intended.
And special thanks to friends, family and community
who have supported and encouraged us on this journey of discovery.

Introducing...

Madonna

Robert

Timothy

William

Samuel

Jackson

Gilbert

Clinton

Bryson

Special appearance by

Mr. Mutton Bird

Dreaming

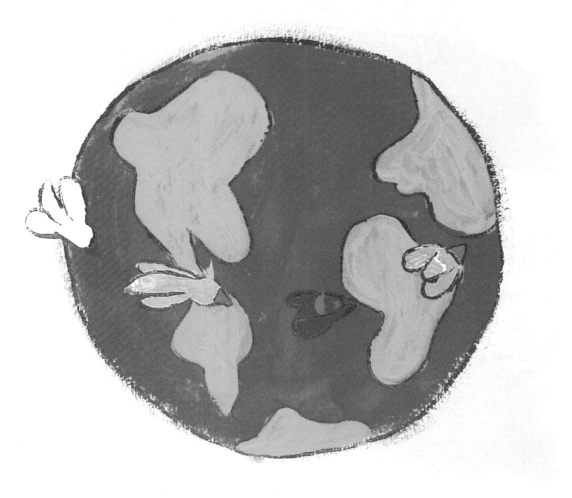

One **beautiful**

spring morning on Russell Island,

nine eggs started to **crack.**

And, one by one,
nine teeny tiny heads

popped out of the eggshells.

One by one, they **looked** around,
and saw each other high in the trees.

And one by one, they became **friends**, except

for Bryson. He was **different**. He was **bossy!**

In fact, he was **born bossy!**

And all that he knew was **bossy!**

He **ruffled** the other bird's feathers

and made them **grumpy.**

The baby birds wanted him out of their friendship group.
But Madonna didn't. Bryson was her brother.
And if he left the group, then so would she.

So it was settled then.
Bryson would stay,

and it would be the nine of them, **together**, as a group.

As the baby birds grew bigger,
it was time for them to learn their lessons.

At first, they stayed together at school
and concentrated on the same subjects:

Leave It Or Eat It?
Hunting
Pecking Order
Friend Or Foe?, and
Understanding Human Speak.

Mr Macaw, the English teacher,

had spent years in a cage kept by the humans.

People had encouraged him to talk.

So now, he used his knowledge to teach other birds.

Mr and Mrs Wagtail came
to the school one day,
and took Madonna away for dance classes.

While Robert went to the
elite **Faster than Raptors
Flying Academy**

three times a week.

He learned how to

soar,

glide,

and his favourite –

Speed flying.

His lessons were very **harsh.**

He spend most of his time

trying to **get away** and **stay safe**

from the flying instructor,

Mr Sea Eagle.

William liked trying out the toys
that people had left lying around on the beach,
and often ended up losing a feather or two,
much to his dislike.

Jackson made friends with a group of humans that sat around and played music and put flowers in their hair.

The nine birds had very different personalities.

But they enjoyed the feeling of
security and **belonging**
that they got from each other in the group.

They always **looked out** for each other.

They sat together
one day and looked about.

Above them was the loud squawking of the
Ritzy Rainbows,

a gang of colourful rainbow lorikeets,
who thought of themselves as the

best looking

birds on the Island!

To the right,
were the **Clownin' Cockies,**
who made **fun** of themselves,
and anyone else nearby by doing **crazy stunts.**
They were often seen
hanging upside down off something!

And on the ground were the

Pushy Plovers,

who were also called the 'Loopy Lapwings',
when they weren't listening.

They were scared of nothing,
and would stand up for themselves,

even against giant foes,

to defend their friends and family.

There were also animal gangs like the
Fur Family,
otherwise known as the Barka Nostra Dogs.

They **chased** cats up trees, and **barked** at the mailman.

And there were the
Pugnacious Pussycats,
who liked a peaceful life,
but supported each other in times of trouble.

It was time for the nine birds
to give their gang a name.

Jackson spoke up first, "The Hippy Chicks!"

"No!" exclaimed William. "That makes us sound
like a bunch girls!"

"I was thinking more of
The Peaceful Doves," said Gilbert.

"We're not DOVES!" growled Bryson,
who had thought
that their name should be the
Follow Bryson Birds.

The discussion ended up being a

shouting match

between the friends, with no one happy.

While the **upset birds** stood with their arms crossed,

a new type of bird appeared on the island.

"Who are you?" asked Madonna.

"I am a Sooty Shearwater,

but you can call me Mr Mutton Bird.
We travel to other countries,
as guided by the weather and the seasons.
It is often a very long flight, but when we get there,
we are met by old friends and we rest and relax,
until it is time to return."

The young birds were fascinated.

"How do you make a nest?" Jackson asked.

"Do you have to be very fit
to fly all that way?" asked Robert.

"What's the outside world like?" William asked.

Mr Mutton Bird smiled.
"You don't always need a **nest** to sleep in—just somewhere
warm and **sheltered**.
And yes, you do need to be

fit and **prepared** for **adventure.**
The world out there is an **amazing** place,
full of **amazing** sights.
There are enough new things out there for you

to fill five lifetimes with **adventures!**"

The birds were **stunned** into silence
by what Mr Mutton Bird had to say.

Eventually, Madonna spoke up.
"Thank you for talking with us.
We hope to see him you again soon."

And with that,

Mr Mutton Bird took off into the sky.

The next morning, Madonna **hopped** and **skipped** and **jumped** about.

"What's gotten you so EXCITED Madonna?" grumbled Bryson,

who was **never** in a good mood.

"I want to tour the world and
live my five lifetimes of adventure!"

"Hmmmm … Mr Mutton Bird had
been very interesting," Timothy said.

"Yes," agreed Jackson.
"Maybe we could ask him to talk to us again?"

Madonna **rolled** her eyes.
"You don't get it do you? Why would we want to hear
of other's adventures, when we can have

adventures of our own?"

"What adventures are there to be had around here that we haven't already done?" asked William.

"Awww…" sighed Madonna. "What I am suggesting is, that WE travel around the world,

and then we can experience all the wonders ourselves."

"It all seems like a lot of work," grumbled Jackson, who was happy with the world as he knew it, and wasn't too interested in putting a lot of effort into changing things.

Robert was all for the idea. It would give him a chance to show off his superior flying skills, and train the others in stamina and distance flying.

One by one the birds agreed that it was a great idea, except Jackson.

But eventually he agreed because he couldn't imagine his life without his friends.

"We could call ourselves The Migrating Birds!" Robert blurted out of nowhere.

"No … I think birds who migrate only go to one country and back," said William.

"Yes … we want to tour all around the world, and go wherever we feel like,' added Madonna.
"Maybe we should go with The Touring Birds?"

The birds broke into chatter amongst themselves, nodding their heads and spreading their wings.

"I recently overheard a conversation about some people that were touring around the world, and the others there called them tourists. How about The Tourist Birds?" Timothy said.

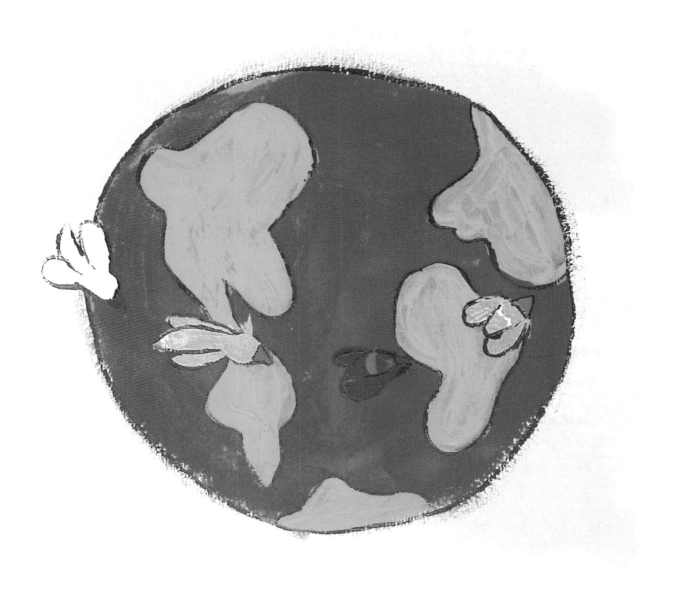

Gilbert, who was very good at negotiating,

knew Madonna would want to use her idea
just because it was hers, but he liked
Timothy's suggestion better.

So, he said to no one in particular,
"I like Touring Birds a lot.
But I think if we called ourselves

The Tourist Birds

it would show us to be intelligent birds

who really know what we are about!"

"Yes" nodded Madonna.
"I like The Tourist Birds.
I was about to suggest it myself!"

The birds all knew that within a short time
Madonna would claim to everyone

that the name was her idea,
and not long afterward,
she would believe it herself.

And from then on,
the nine bird friends called themselves

The Tourist Birds.

Now, all they had to do was

to **prepare** themselves,

leave home,

and let the

adventure begin.

Russell Island Fact File

Location: Sandwiched between the mainland of Australia and North Stradbroke Island in the state of Queensland.

Size: Eight kilometres long (north-to-south) and nearly three kilometres wide.

Population: 2, 473   (2011)

Named After: Lord John Russell, the Secretary of State for the Colonies in the 1840s.

First Settlers: Europeans in 1866. Farmers and oystermen were the first full-time inhabitants, but with the arrival of the Jackson family in 1906, a small village was created on the western side of the island called Jacksonville. There was a sawmill, pineapple canning factory, jetty and a picture theatre.

School: Yes. It opened in 1916.

Services: Police station, supermarket, butcher, post office, service station, vet, medical practice, chemist, hairdresser, bakery, landscape centre, lawyer, library, and public pool.

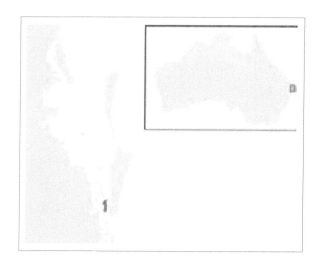

Barka Nostra
home turf

Turtle Wetlands

Sandy Beach

Sailing and kayaking

Primary School

Ferry
dock.

Shops

Russell Island

Swimming pool

Pugnacious Cats
Home turf

Tourist Birds home

Tourist Birds school

Old Ferry dock

Shopping/busin
Residential
Bushland
Beach

About the Authors

Tom

Jenni

Tom and Jenni were both born in New Zealand.
Tom moved to Australia in 2003 and Jenni in 2006.
They moved to Russell Island, Queensland, after
working in the hot centre of Australia.
Amongst the bounty of entertaining wildlife on Russell Island,
Tom and Jenni have found themselves
in the unexpected position of new careers as a writer and artist.

CPSIA information can be obtained at www.ICGtesting.com
Printed in the USA
LVOW01s1019051214

5898LVAU00003B/6/P

9 780994 204417